First published in hardback in Great Britain
by Andersen Press Ltd in 2002
First published in paperback by Collins Picture Books in 2003

1 3 5 7 9 10 8 6 4 2

ISBN: 000-714567-5

Collins Picture Books is an imprint of the Children's Division,
part of HarperCollins Publishers Ltd.

Text and illustrations copyright © Colin McNaughton 2002

The author/illustrator asserts the moral right to be identified
as the author/illustrator of the work.

A CIP catalogue record for this title is available from
the British Library.

The HarperCollins website address is: www.fireandwater.com

Printed and bound in Hong Kong

Colin McNaughton

S.W.A.L.K.

Collins

An imprint of HarperCollins*Publishers*

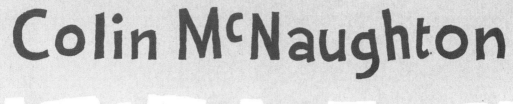

Preston's got a girlfriend,
Preston's got a girlfriend.

Early one morning, just as the sun was rising, Preston was woken by a commotion in the garden below.

Preston's dad and Postman Paté were dancing round the garden singing: "Preston's got a girlfriend, Preston's got a girlfriend." Preston's mum told them off for being silly and handed Preston a letter.

"It's from that little girl you met at the seaside," said Preston's mum.

"Max!" he cried. "How do you know?"

"The postmark," said Preston's mum.

"And… because it says 'S.W.A.L.K.' on the back."

"S.W.A.L.K?" said Preston.

"Sealed With A Loving Kiss," said Preston's mum.

"Oh," said Preston.

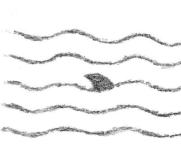

Preston opened the letter and this is what it said:

Dear Preston, hello! Life here at the seaside is really boring now you're not here to play with. Same old thing every day—sun, sea and sand. I miss you like stink! Please can you write to me and tell me all about yourself?

Preston picked up a pencil
and paper and began to write…

Dear Max,

Hi! Thank you for your letter.

So, you want to know all about me?

Okey-dokey, here goes –

My mum is very sensible
but she is always cuddling me.

My dad likes gardening
and is very silly.

My mum works as a dinner lady
and my dad is a carpenter.

Every day I get up,

get washed,

get dressed,

get fed,

and set off for school.

On my way to school I walk through the woods. I like to listen to the birds singing.

At school I have a lot of friends.

We like football and books the best.

Our teacher is called Miss Thump
and she tells me off a lot.

She is quite nice but she gives us far too much hard work.

Sometimes we have music.

Sometimes we have maths.

Sometimes we write stories,

and sometimes we have art.

Lunchtime is my favourite time of day because my mum is the dinner lady!

Most of the time, though,
I just sit at my desk and daydream.

After school, I sometimes go to
the park. (But not very often because
Billy the Bully is usually there.)

Sometimes I go to the
shops for my mum.

Sometimes I go to see my dad
to help him with his work.

Sometimes I visit my granny.

She is about a million years old

and is not very strong.

And at bedtime my mum
or my dad read to me.

As you can see, nothing much
happens around here. I'm going
to stop writing now so I can
catch the post.

Please write back soon, Max.

Love Preston.

X X X (Kisses on the bottom – tee hee.)

Collect all the Preston Pig Stories

0-00-714013-4

0-00-714011-8

0-00-714014-2

0-00-714015-0

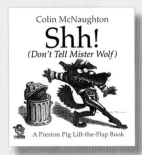

0-00-664715-4

0-00-714012-6

0-00-712635-2

0-00-713235-2

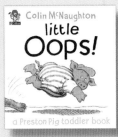

0-00-713236-0

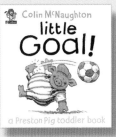

0-00-713234-4

0-00-713237-9

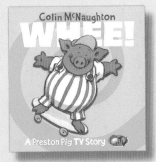

0-00-712371-X

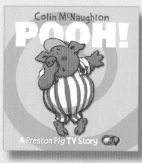

0-00-712370-1

0-00-712372-8

Colin McNaughton is one of Britain's most highly-acclaimed picture book talents and a winner of many prestigious awards. His Preston Pig Stories are hugely successful with Preston now starring in his own animated television series on CITV.